Fun and Bumps

In these stories you will meet:

Thomas

Bill and Ben

Fergus

Rusty

Elizabeth

The Fat
Controller

And these more difficult words:

trains   lorry

DEAN

Book Band: Yellow

Lexile® measure: 250L

First published in Great Britain in 2016
This Reading Ladder edition published 2018 by Dean,
an imprint of Egmont UK Limited,
The Yellow Building, 1 Nicholas Road, London W11 4AN

Thomas the Tank Engine & Friends™

CREATED BY BRITT ALLCROFT

HiT entertainment

ISBN 978 1 4052 8258 1
www.egmont.co.uk
A CIP catalogue record for this title is available from the British Library.
Printed in China
70244/001

Stay safe online. Egmont is not responsible for content hosted by third parties.

Egmont takes its responsibility to the planet and its inhabitants very seriously.
We aim to use papers from well-managed forests run by responsible suppliers.

Series consultant: Nikki Gamble

Fun and Bumps

This is Fergus.
Fergus is good.

Fergus had a big job to do with Bill and Ben.

I have a big job, Thomas!

Bill and Ben did not want to do jobs.

We want fun!

9

Bump, bump, bump went Bill.

Grin, grin, grin went Ben.

Bill and Ben went to get a rock crusher.

Bill and Ben got the rock crusher. They went bump, bump, bump.

Fergus told them to go slow.

Bump, bump, bump.
They did not go slow.

Rocks fell. Crash!

Fergus was stuck. Now Bill and Ben had a big job. They did not bump. They did not grin. They did the job.

Bill and Ben did a good job.
Fergus was free.

Tracks to Fix

This is Rusty. Rusty is good at his jobs.

RUSTY

5

Rusty had a job to do.
He needed to fix some
tracks. He had two
trains to help him.

It was a big job.
There was a lot to do.

But there was too much to do.

Rusty needed help. He needed a lorry.

Elizabeth the lorry was strong.

Elizabeth the
lorry and Rusty
did the job.

RUSTY

5

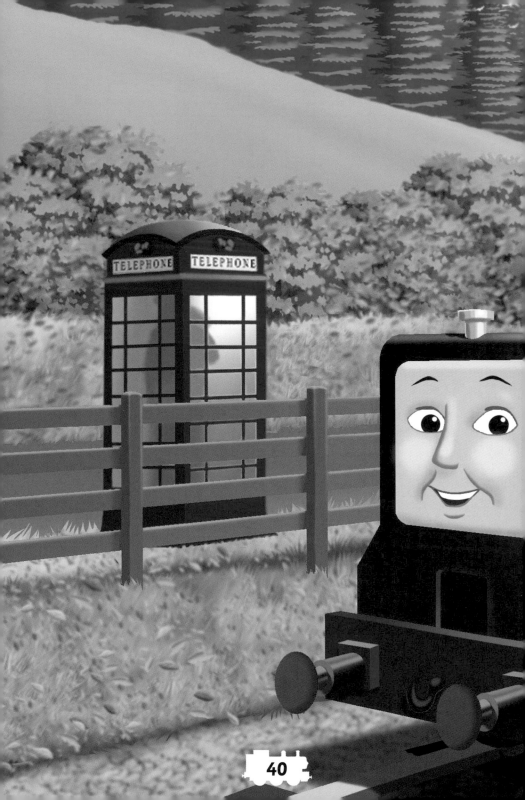

Rusty went to tell
The Fat Controller.

Rusty and Elizabeth are good at jobs.

Mix and Match

Bill and Ben like to bump.
Follow the bumpy lines with
your finger to match the
words to the vehicles.

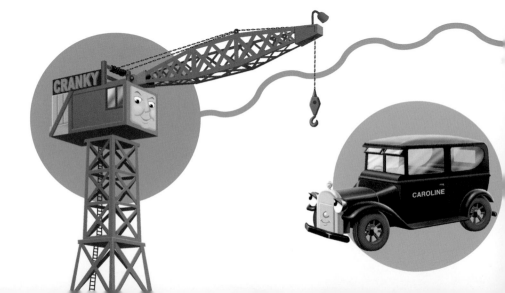

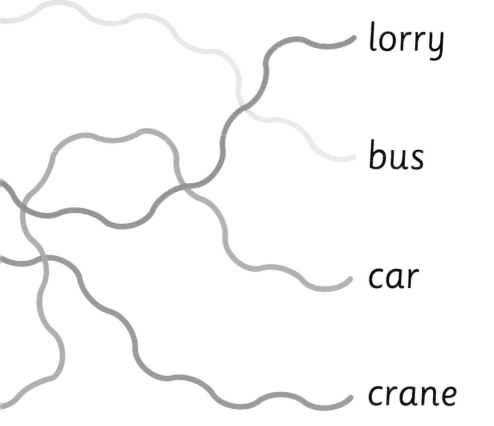

lorry

bus

car

crane

Big 'b' Challenge

Point to all the vehicles which start with a 'b' sound.